KT-363-842

KOALA CALAMITY

SURF'S UP

JONATHAN MERES

Illustrated by Neal Layton

HarperCollins *Children's Books*

First published in Great Britain by HarperCollins *Children's Books* in 2013
HarperCollins *Children's Books* is a division of HarperCollins*Publishers* Ltd,
77-85 Fulham Palace Road, Hammersmith, London, W6 8JB.

The HarperCollins website address is:
www.harpercollins.co.uk

1

Text copyright © Jonathan Meres 2013
Illustrations copyright © Neal Layton 2013

ISBN 978-0-00-749081-3

Jonathan Meres and Neal Layton assert the moral right to be
identified as the author and illustrator of this work.

Printed and bound in England by Clays Ltd, St Ives plc

Conditions of Sale
This book is sold subject to the condition that it shall not, by way of
trade or otherwise, be lent, re-sold, hired out or otherwise circulated without
the publisher's prior consent in any form, binding or cover other than that in
which it is published and without a similar condition including this condition
being imposed on the subsequent purchaser. All rights reserved.

MIX
**Paper from
responsible sources**
FSC C007454

FSC™ is a non-profit international organisation established to promote
the responsible management of the world's forests. Products carrying the
FSC label are independently certified to assure consumers that they come
from forests that are managed to meet the social, economic and
ecological needs of present and future generations,
and other controlled sources.

Find out more about HarperCollins and the environment at
www.harpercollins.co.uk/green

To Romi and Theo

Meet...

Dude

Squirt

Bro

The
CRAZIEST
koalas
in town!

and Squeak

Chapter One

Days rarely started with a bang at The Acacia Koala Sanctuary and today was no different. All was spookily quiet. The only thing rising was the sun. The sky in the east was gradually changing from inky black to pinky blue. Not that Dude, or Bro, or Squirt noticed. Dude, Bro and Squirt were still fast asleep, along with all the other koalas. Well, all the other koalas except one.

"Wakey, wakey!" squeaked Squeak. "Wakey, wakey!"

Dude, Bro and Squirt slept blissfully on. Not only were the koalas naturally very lazy and sleepy, they'd been up unusually late the night before, giggling and chomping eucalyptus branches high in the treetops. It was still quite a new experience for Squirt to be allowed to hang out with his big brother, Bro, and Bro's best friend, Dude. It was something Squirt thought would never ever happen.

But the adventure they'd had finding their way across the city to the big zoo had changed all that. Without Squirt, Dude and Bro would never have made it. Since then, Squirt had no longer irritated his brother and got on his nerves *all* the time. Just *most* of the time.

"Wakey, wakey!" squeaked Squeak again. "Wakey, wakey! Wakey, wakey!"

Bro let out a little snore. Dude yawned. Squirt scratched himself. But all three remained determinedly asleep.

Squeak wasn't very happy. *She* was awake and couldn't see why everyone else wasn't awake too. Sleeping was boring. Especially when there were so many other things to do. Like bounce up and down on her big brother's tummy, for instance.

"Uh? What?" grunted Bro, finally beginning to wake up. "What's going on? Get off me, Squeak, ya big fat wombat!"

"Wakey, wakey!" squeaked Squeak. "Wakey, wakey, wakey!"

"All right, all right," said Bro. "I heard you the first time."

"Heh-heh-heh," chuckled Dude, despite still being half asleep.

"You can put a sock in it too, ya wallaby," said Bro. "Sorry, mate," said Dude, stifling a yawn.

Bro could be pretty grumpy at the best of times. And now wasn't exactly the best of times. Not only had he been woken up by his little sister using his tummy as a trampoline, he'd been in the middle of a particularly nice dream in which he'd been chowing down *the* most delicious eucalyptus branch he'd ever tasted.

"Morning, sis," said Squirt.

"Yeah! Squirty-wirty, Squirty-wirty!" squeaked Squeak, throwing herself at Squirt and very nearly knocking him off the branch. For a small koala, Squeak could be surprisingly strong at times.

"Careful!" said Squirt.

"Poo, poo!" replied Squeak.

"Heh-heh-heh," chuckled Dude again, by now somewhere between half asleep and half awake.

"So *that's* where you are!" said Mrs M, appearing in the treetop. "What are you doing up here? It's much too high!"

"Sorry, Ma," said Squirt.

"Not you, Squirt," said Mrs M. "I meant

your sister!"

"Oh, right!" said Squirt. Not only was he not used to hanging out with Dude and Bro high in the treetops, he still wasn't used to not being the youngest. He didn't *mind* not being the youngest – he *loved* it! It meant he was no longer constantly teased and treated like a baby.

"Morning, Mrs M," said Dude, finally fully awake. Or as awake as Dude ever was, anyway.

"Morning, Dude," said Mrs M. "Morning, dear."

But Bro said nothing. Either he'd fallen asleep again, or he was cross because he hated it when his mum called him dear.

15

Just like Squirt hated being called Squirty-wirty. By his mum, that is.

"Listen up," announced Mrs M, "I've got something important to tell you."

"What is it, Ma?" said Squirt.

"Your father and I have to go away."

"Away?" said Squirt, suddenly anxious.

"Not for long," laughed Mrs M. "I've just got to go and see Aunt Jemima for a while, that's all."

Aunt Jemima was Mrs M's sister. She lived in another part of The Acacia Koala Sanctuary altogether.

"But…" began Squirt.

"But, what?" said Mrs M.

"Who'll look after Squeak?"

"You will," answered Mrs M.

"Me?" said Squirt.

"Yeah! Squirty-wirty! Squirty-wirty!" squeaked Squeak, bouncing up and down.

"Heh-heh-heh," chuckled Bro.

"And you will too, dear," said Mrs M.

That shut Bro up. "Me?"

"Yeah! Bro-bro! Bro-bro!" squeaked Squeak.

"Heh-heh-heh," chuckled Dude.

"All three of you will," said Mrs M.

"Yeah! Dudey-wudey! Dudey-wudey!" squeaked Squeak.

That shut Dude up too.

"Do we *have* to, Ma?" grunted Bro.

"Yes, you have to," said Mrs M. "She's

your sister!"

"Exactly!" said Bro. He wasn't happy. First he'd been woken from his slumbers, and now this? How much worse could things get?

"When was the last time I asked you to do something?" said Mrs M. "Actually *do* something?"

Bro thought for a moment. He couldn't remember the last time his mum had asked him to do something, but that wasn't the point. The point was he'd got better things to do today than look after his pesky little sister. Like sleep. And chow down a few juicy eucy branches. And catch a few rays.

"Well?" insisted Mrs M.

"Erm…" said Bro.

"Precisely," said Mrs M. "It's high time you boys started to help out a bit and show some responsibility!"

Squirt wasn't entirely sure what responsibility was, but whatever it was, it sounded very grown-up and important. "I don't mind, Mum."

"Creep," muttered Bro, glaring at Squirt.

"You're a good boy, Squirty-wirty," said Mrs M.

"Please don't call me that, Mum," said Squirt through gritted teeth.

"You coming or what, Mrs M?" called Mr M from somewhere down below.

Mrs M smiled. "I'd better go before he

falls asleep again!"

"I know how he feels," muttered Bro.

"Heh-heh-heh," chuckled Dude.

"Coming, Mr M!" called Mrs M.

"Mummy, bye-bye! Mummy, bye-bye!"
squeaked Squeak, flinging herself at Mrs M.

"Bye-bye, Squeaky-weaky," laughed Mrs M. "You be a good girl, now. And you boys behave yourselves!"

"We will!" said Squirt. "Won't we, guys?"

"What?" said Bro. "Oh, yeah."

"Totally, mate," said Dude. "Totally."

"Good," said Mrs M, disentangling herself from Squeak's clutches. "We'll be back by nightfall."

And with that, Mrs M was gone, leaving Squirt, Dude, Bro and Squeak alone in the treetop once more.

"Talking of nightfall," said Bro, stretching and yawning.

"Heh-heh-heh," chuckled Dude, doing exactly the same.

Squirt couldn't believe his eyes. "You're not going back to sleep, are you?"

"Too right I am, mate," said Bro. "Unless you've got any better ideas?"

"But…" began Squirt.

"But, what?" said Bro.

"We're supposed to be looking after Squeak!" said Squirt.

"Oi, less of the *we*," said Bro, wedging himself firmly between a couple of branches and closing his eyes.

"What do you mean?" asked Squirt.

"Well, you're the one who said you didn't mind," said Bro.

"So?" said Squirt.

"So *you* look after her!" replied Bro.

"Me?" said Squirt.

"Yeah!" said Squeak, launching herself at Squirt and bouncing up and down on him. "Squirty-wirty! Squirty-wirty!"

"Heh-heh-heh," chuckled Dude.

"Yeah!" said Squeak, turning her attention to Dude and bouncing up and down on him instead. "Dudey-wudey! Dudey-wudey!"

"Heh-heh-heh," chuckled Bro, before stopping suddenly and glaring at his baby sister. "Don't even *think* about bouncing on me!"

Squeak stopped bouncing. "What are we doing?"

"Well, I dunno about you guys, but

I know what *I'm* doing," said Bro, wedging himself even more firmly between the branches and closing his eyes even more tightly.

"Poo, poo!" said Squeak indignantly.

Bro sighed. It didn't look like he was going to get much kip as long as Squeak was around. He needed to think of something for her to do. Something to keep her busy for as long as possible. But what?

"Poo, poo!" squeaked Squeak again, bouncing up and down. "Poo, poo! Poo, poo!"

Bro cranked open an eye and looked at his sister. Where on earth did she get all that energy from? Had *he* been like that

when *he* was a baby? Surely not! And then suddenly it hit him – the perfect way to tire Squeak out!

"Hey, Squeak," said Bro. "Wanna have some fun?"

"Yeah!" squeaked Squeak. "Fun, fun, funny fun!"

"OK," said Bro. "Find the tallest tree you can."

"And then?" said Squeak.

"Climb as high as you can," said Bro.

"And then?" said Squeak.

"Get a leaf," said Bro.

"And then?" said Squeak.

"Bring it back," said Bro.

"And then?" said Squeak.

Bro thought for a moment. "And then I'll think of something else."

"Erm…" said Squirt.

"What?" grunted Bro, getting grumpier and grumpier.

"I'm not sure that's a very good idea," said Squirt.

"Oh, yeah?" replied Bro. "Well, I think it's a great idea. What do *you* think, mate?"

Dude didn't reply straightaway. In fact, Dude didn't reply at all. Not because he couldn't think what to say, but because he'd fallen asleep again, which only made Bro even grumpier. It was *his* idea. It was him who should have fallen asleep again first!

"Squeak?" said Squirt, looking round. "Where are you?"

But it was too late. Squeak had already gone.

Chapter Two

Squirt woke, not so much with a start, but more like the beginning of a start. Something didn't feel quite right. In fact, something felt definitely wrong. But what? Squirt couldn't quite put his finger on it. Or his claw on it anyway.

He gave himself a nice, long scratch. Not only was scratching just about the best feeling in the whole wide world, it also helped Squirt to think. The effect was almost instant. Squirt suddenly remembered something. This wasn't the first time he'd woken up today – it was the *second* time.

Something nearby snored. Squirt looked round to see Dude and Bro, both fast asleep and cuddling each other. Squirt looked again. *Odd*, he thought. Dude appeared to be nibbling one of Bro's ears.

"Ouch!" yelled Bro, waking up suddenly and swatting Dude as if he was some kind of overgrown fly. "Gerroff me, ya big fat wallaby! You just bit my ear!"

"Aw, sorry about that, mate," said Dude.

"I should think so too," grumbled Bro.

"I was just having this really weird dream," explained Dude.

"Oh, yeah?" said Bro, not terribly interested.

"Yeah," said Dude. "Dreamed I was eating a great big furry eucy branch."

Bro looked at Dude. "That wasn't a eucy branch! That was my ear!"

"Oh, right," said Dude. "No wonder it didn't taste very nice."

Squirt couldn't help giggling.

"It's not funny," muttered Bro under his breath.

"Heh-heh-heh," chuckled Dude. "It's a *bit* funny, mate."

Bro thought for a moment. "S'pose you're right, mate. It is a *bit* funny. But only a bit."

Dude didn't reply. He'd noticed something. Something very important. Something that the other two hadn't noticed yet. "Where's Squeak?"

"What?" said Bro.

"Yer baby sister."

"I *know* who Squeak is!" said Bro.

"So where is she, Bro?"

Squirt gasped. So *that's* what was wrong – Squeak wasn't there! They'd been left in charge of her and what had they done? They'd fallen asleep on the job!

"Oops," said Bro.

"*Oops?*" said Squirt. "This is more than just *oops*!"

"Ya reckon?" said Bro.

"Er, yes, I do, actually," said Squirt. "If we've lost her we're in trouble. *Big* trouble!"

"Ya reckon?" said Bro.

"Yes, I *do* reckon!" said Squirt. "She's just a baby! She's way too young to be wandering about all by herself! Anything could happen!"

"Ya reckon?" said Bro.

"Can you please stop saying that?" said Squirt. "It's getting *really* annoying!"

"Ya reckon?" said Bro.

Squirt sighed. This wasn't good. They were *supposed* to be showing some responsibility, whatever *that* was. "Mum and Dad are going to go bonkers when they find out!"

"*If* they find out," said Dude.

Squirt looked at Dude for a moment. "You're right!" he said.

Dude was surprised. "I am?"

"Yes," said Squirt. "If Mum and Dad

don't find out, then they won't go bonkers, will they?"

"So what are you saying?" said Bro.

"I'm saying we have to find her!" said Squirt impatiently. "*And quickly!*"

"Aw, you're joking," said Bro.

Squirt looked at his big brother in disbelief. Joking? He'd never been more serious in his life!

"How about we have another kip – and *then* find her?" said Bro.

"No! We have to find her *now*!" said Squirt. "It's all your fault anyway!"

Bro was confused. "My fault? How d'ya work that out?"

"Easy," said Squirt. "*You're* the one who

told her to go and climb the tallest tree she could find, just so you could get some more sleep!"

"The little feller's right, mate," said Dude. "You did."

Bro shot Dude a look. "Whose side are you on?"

"I'm just saying, mate," said Dude.

"Well, don't, mate," said Bro.

"Stop squabbling, you two!" said Squirt. "We've got to find her! Now!"

Dude and Bro looked at each other.

"He's right again, mate," said Dude.

Bro nodded. "I know he is, mate."

Dude and Bro turned round again. But Squirt had disappeared down below.

"Let's go," said Dude, almost sounding urgent.

Bro sighed deeply. "Coming."

Squirt was smaller than Dude and Bro. He was also much quicker at climbing down trees. By the time Dude and Bro got to the bottom, Squirt was scampering across the ground just as fast as his little legs could carry him.

"Stop!" yelled Bro.

"Totally!" yelled Dude.

Squirt stopped until Dude and Bro caught up with him.

"Where are you going?" panted Bro.

"To the highest tree!" said Squirt. "That's where you told Squeak to go, remember!"

"Aw, yeah," said Bro, remembering.

"You said, 'Climb to the top of the tallest tree and get a leaf ','" said Squirt.

"And then?" said Bro.

"'Bring it back'," replied Squirt.

"And then?" asked Bro.

"You said you'd think of something else," said Squirt, beginning to get exasperated.

"I did?" said Bro.

Squirt sighed. "You did!"

"Heh-heh-heh," chuckled Dude.

"What are you laughing at?" said Bro.

Dude thought for a moment. "I've got no idea, mate."

Squirt looked up. From down on the ground all the trees in The Acacia Koala

Sanctuary looked pretty tall to him, but which one was the tallest? It was hard to say. And then he saw it. One tree just a little bit higher than all the rest.

"Look," said Squirt. "Over there!"

Dude and Bro both looked.

"Do you think that one's the tallest?" said Squirt.

"Could be," said Dude.

"Ya reckon?" said Bro.

"Don't start *that* again!" said Squirt, scurrying towards the tree to get a better look.

"Does that look like a eucy tree to you, mate?" said Bro, setting off after Squirt again.

"Nah, mate," said Dude, following. "Wish it was!"

"That makes two of us," said Bro.

"Two?" said Dude. "Who's the other one?"

"Me, ya wombat!" said Bro.

"Oh, right, yeah," said Dude.

By the time Dude and Bro reached the tree, Squirt was already halfway up it.

"Squeak? You up there?" called Squirt. "Squeak?"

But there was no reply. Squirt began to get more and more worried. What could have happened to Squeak? He had to keep climbing. He *had* to get to the top of the tree as soon as possible!

Squirt climbed and climbed and climbed. Far below, the everyday sounds of the sanctuary faded first to a whisper and then to nothing at all. The only sound to be heard was the sound of Dude and Bro puffing and panting (and grumbling, in Bro's case) as they followed him up the tree.

Then, all of a sudden, Squirt could climb no further. Not because he'd finally run out of puff, but because he'd finally run out of tree. He'd reached the very top of the very highest tree in The Acacia Koala Sanctuary. The view was quite simply breathtaking. In one direction, Squirt could see the sprawling city. In the other direction, he could see green mountains and a splash of bright blue ocean. But Squirt couldn't see the one thing that he really wanted to see – his baby sister, Squeak.

"She up here?" puffed Bro as he and Dude eventually appeared at the top of the tree.

No," said Squirt.

"Oh," said Bro.

"Bummer," said Dude.

There was nothing much else to be said. Well, there was *one* more thing to be said. It was just a question of who was going to say it first.

Dude, Bro and Squirt looked at each other.

Each knew what the other two were thinking.

"Well?" said Bro.

"Well?" said Dude.

"Well?" said Squirt.

There was a moment's pause. The wind began to stir the leaves. The branches began to sway ever so slightly. Somewhere even higher above, an aeroplane drew a thick white line across the sky.

"What now?" said Dude, Bro and Squirt together.

Chapter Three

"Are you thinking what I'm thinking, mate?" said Dude.

"I've no idea, mate," said Bro.

"What do you mean?" said Dude.

"How am I supposed to know what you're thinking?" said Bro.

"Uh?" said Dude.

"Think about it," said Bro.

"Think about what?" said Dude.

"What I just said," said Bro.

Dude thought about it. Or at least he tried to. "Sorry, mate. Can't remember."

"You can't remember what?" said Bro.

Squirt sighed with exasperation. Here they were, at the very top of the very highest tree in The Acacia Koala Sanctuary – on a mission of the utmost importance – and Dude and Bro were making even less sense than usual. And *that* was saying something.

"Can I ask a question, please?" said Squirt.

"Go for it," said Bro.

"Totally, mini-dude," said Dude.

"What on earth are you two talking about?"

Dude and Bro turned to each other and shrugged. Even they had no idea what they were talking about any more.

"I'm off!" said Squirt, making his way back down the tree again.

"Where to?" said Bro.

"Well, she's obviously not up here," said Squirt. "So she must be somewhere else!"

"Who?" said Bro.

"*Who do you think?*" yelled Squirt, disappearing from view. "Squeak!"

"All right, all right," said Bro, following. "Keep yer fur on!"

Dude thought about chuckling, but decided not to. It was probably best just to concentrate on climbing back down the tree. They were so high up, one false move could spell disaster. Not that Dude actually *knew* how to spell disaster, or any other word for that matter.

"Which way now?" said Squirt to himself, when he eventually reached the ground again.

"Which way to where?" said a familiar voice.

Squirt looked around, but couldn't see where the voice was coming from.

"Wah, ha ha ha ha!" screeched the voice. "Up here!"

Squirt looked up to see Kylie the kookaburra sitting on the branch of a neighbouring tree.

"Oh, it's you," he said.

"Are you sure?" said Kylie.

"Am I sure what?" said Squirt.

"Are you sure it's me?" said Kylie, before bursting out laughing like it was the best joke ever.

But Squirt was in no mood for jokes. He only had one thing on his mind. To find his baby sister as soon as possible, before she came to any harm. And – before his mum and dad came back and he, Dude and Bro got into big, big trouble!

"Have you seen my sister?" asked Squirt.

"Who?" said Kylie.

"Squeak!" said Squirt.

Kylie squeaked.

"What are you doing?" asked Squirt.

"You told me to squeak," said Kylie. "So I squeaked!"

"That's not what I meant!" said Squirt. "I meant I'm *looking* for Squeak!"

"I can't hear you," laughed Kylie. "You'll have to squeak up!"

"What?" said Squirt blankly.

"Wah, ha ha ha ha!" cackled Kylie. "D'ya get it? You'll have to *squeak* up?"

Squirt had forgotten just how annoying Kylie could be – and right now Kylie was being very annoying indeed! What with that and Dude and Bro continually talking gibberish, it looked like it was going to be a long day.

Right on cue, Dude and Bro finally appeared.

"Oh, it's you," said Bro when he saw Kylie.

"Are you sure?" said Kylie.

Bro looked confused. "Am I sure what?"

"Are you sure it's me?" said Kylie, before bursting out laughing.

"Heh-heh-heh," chuckled Dude.

Squirt sighed. "So have you seen her or not?"

"Who?" said Kylie.

"My little sister!" shouted Squirt. "Squeak!"

"That's your sister?" said Kylie. "Squeak?"

"Yes!" said Squirt, through gritted teeth.

"Why didn't you say so in the first place?" said Kylie.

Squirt looked at Kylie for a moment. "So, have you seen her, then?"

"Oh, yes, I've seen her," said Kylie. "Funny-looking little thing, isn't she?"

"Oi, do you mind?" said Bro. "That's my sister you're talking about!"

"No," said Kylie.

"No what?" said Bro.

"No, I don't mind that it's your sister I'm talking about," said Kylie.

"Heh-heh-heh," chuckled Dude.

"Don't *you* start," said Bro.

"Sorry, mate," said Dude.

"STOP!" yelled Squirt at the top of his voice.

Dude, Bro and Kylie all turned and looked at Squirt.

"Have you, or have you not, seen my little sister, Squeak?" said Squirt to Kylie.

"Yes, I have," said Kylie.

Brilliant, thought Squirt. This was a bit more promising. Now if only Kylie would say when and where she'd seen Squeak, they could go and find her. They'd be back in their own treetop in next to no time. Mum and Dad would be none the wiser.

"When?" said Squirt.

"Not long ago," replied Kylie.

Not long ago, thought Squirt. This was good. Squeak couldn't be all that far away, then. She was only little, after all. How far could a little koala actually get? The Acacia Koala Sanctuary was big, but it wasn't *that* big. Not like the enormous zoo on the other side of the city where they'd all gone for a holiday that time. Now that really *was* big! The adventures he and Dude and Bro had had finding Mum and Dad were enough to make your tail curl! Even a koala's tiny stump of a tail! No, if Squeak was lost in the *big* zoo, she could be wandering around for days before anyone found her. But here in The Acacia Koala Sanctuary? Well, there were only so many places you could actually go.

"Kylie, where did you see Squeak?" said Squirt.

"Here," said Kylie.

"Here?" said Squirt. "Right here?"

"Right here," repeated Kylie.

"Whoa," said Bro.

"Awesome," said Dude.

"Did you speak to her?" asked Squirt.

"Kind of," said Kylie.

Kind of? thought Squirt. *Kind of?* What was *that* supposed to mean? You either speak to someone or you don't! Getting a straightforward answer from Kylie was like getting a kangaroo to stop bouncing. It was just about impossible!

"Look," said Squirt, "we really need to know what she said. And we really need to know *now*! So if you wouldn't mind just—"

"Big tree!" blurted Kylie. "Big tree! Big tree!"

"What?" said Squirt.

"That's what she kept saying," said Kylie. "Big tree! Big tree!"

Of course, thought Squirt. That made sense.

"At least I think that's what she was saying," said Kylie. "She was hopping about so much it was hard to tell."

"Heh-heh-heh," chuckled Bro.

"Heh-heh-heh," echoed Dude.

Squirt shot Dude and Bro a disapproving look. This was clearly no laughing matter.

"Sorry, mate," said Bro.

"Totally," said Dude.

"Then what?" continued Squirt.

"I told her," explained Kylie.

"You told her what?" said Squirt.

"I told her where the big tree is," said Kylie.

Fantastic! thought Squirt. Maybe they hadn't been up the highest tree in the sanctuary after all. There must be an even higher one somewhere else. And that must be where Squeak was! If only this bonkers bird would hurry up and tell them where they could find it.

"Where is the big tree?" said Squirt.

"In the forest," said Kylie.

"Which forest?" said Squirt, trying not to lose his temper.

"The one where my cousin Kyle lives," said Kylie.

"And where's that?" said Squirt, beginning to get more and more agitated.

"Next to the beach," said Kylie.

"The beach?" squeaked Squirt.

"The beach?" said Bro and Dude, together.

"The beach!" said Kylie again, bobbing up and down excitedly. "The beach, the beach, the beach!"

"Which beach?" said Squirt.

"Wah, ha ha ha ha!" laughed Kylie. "The beach next to the ocean!"

"The ocean?" said Bro.

"Which ocean?" said Dude.

"Wah, ha ha ha ha! *Which ocean?*" screeched Kylie. "Now that's what I call funny!"

There was one more question Squirt had to ask, but he hardly dared. He had a horrible feeling he already knew what the answer was.

"What happened next?"

"Mate, she was off like a rocket!" said Kylie. "Couldn't see her for dust!"

Squirt couldn't believe it. "And you let her go? Just like that?"

"I couldn't have stopped her if I'd wanted to!" said Kylie.

Squirt sighed. There was no point getting angry with Kylie. Finding Squeak was way more important. And it was beginning to look like that wasn't going to be quite as straightforward as he had hoped.

Chapter Four

"Come on, you two!" said Squirt, shooting back up the same tree they'd come down just a few minutes earlier.

Bro sighed wearily. "Aw, mate, do we have to? I'm whacked!"

"Do you want to see your baby sister again?" called Squirt.

Bro pulled a face. "What kind of a dumb question is that? Course I do!"

"In that case, you'd better follow me!" yelled Squirt, disappearing further and further up into the branches.

Dude and Bro looked at each other and shrugged. Koalas might be fantastic climbers, but that didn't mean they always *wanted* to climb. Right then Dude and Bro would have liked nothing better than to have kicked back, chowed down a couple of eucalyptus branches and caught a few rays. But they knew they shouldn't.

"The little feller's right, Bro," said Dude.

"I know he is, Dude," said Bro reluctantly.

"After you, Bro," said Dude, waiting for Bro to begin climbing.

"No, after you, Dude," said Bro. "I insist."

"Wah, ha ha ha ha!" laughed Kylie loudly, giving Dude and Bro such a fright that they *both* shot straight up the tree at the same time.

"Wah, ha ha ha ha!" laughed Kylie again. "Missing you already!"

"Crazy bird," muttered Bro under his breath.

"Heh-heh-heh," chuckled Dude.

"Hurry up!" called Squirt. "We haven't got a moment to lose!"

Puffing and panting, Dude and Bro

eventually found Squirt clinging to a branch and gazing into the distance.

"Can you see anything Squirt?" said Dude.

"I can see lots of things!" said Squirt.

"But can you see the big tree?" asked Dude.

"No," said Squirt, scanning the horizon. "I can see the ocean, though."

"Cool," said Dude.

"Yeah," agreed Bro. "And wet."

"Heh-heh-heh," chuckled Dude. "Good one, Bro."

"Can you two please be serious for a minute?" said Squirt, glaring at Dude and Bro. "We've got to get out of this place and find Squeak."

"How are we going to do that?" said Dude.

"Easy," replied Squirt, scampering along the branch. "Follow me."

Bro sighed. "Not again."

"Yes, again!" insisted Squirt. "Are you coming or not?"

"Do we have a choice?" asked Bro.

"Not really," said Squirt, setting off again, even faster.

Dude and Bro looked at each other before running after Squirt. They expected him to stop when he got to the end of the branch, but he didn't. He simply leaped into thin air!

"Wheeeeeee!" squealed Squirt.

Dude and Bro were horrified.

"Squirt?" yelled Bro. "Where are you?"

"Whoa!" said Dude. "He's, like, totally vanished, Bro!"

"I'm sorry, Squirt!" yelled Bro. "For everything!"

"Over here!" yelled a voice.

Dude and Bro looked in the direction

of the voice. There, in the next tree, was Squirt, sitting on a branch.

"Are you joking?" said Bro. "You actually expect us to *jump*?"

"Of course!" said Squirt.

"Through the air?" said Bro.

"What else are you going to jump through?" said Squirt.

"But…" began Bro.

Squirt looked at his big brother for a moment. "You're not *scared*, are you?"

"No!" said Bro indignantly. "What makes you think that?"

"Heh-heh-heh," chuckled Dude.

"I don't know what you're laughing at, Dude," said Bro. "You've got to do it too."

Dude immediately stopped chuckling. "Aw, yeah," he said.

"Come on!" yelled Squirt. "It's easy-peasy!"

"Easy-peasy, lemon-squeezy?" said Dude. "Or just easy-peasy?"

Squirt sighed impatiently. Dude and Bro were wasting valuable time. And time was something they didn't have a lot of at the moment. Squeak could be anywhere by now. They needed to find her as quickly as possible, before she came to any harm!

"Are you two going to jump, or what?"

Dude and Bro looked at each other.

"After you, Bro," said Dude.

"No, after you, Dude," said Bro.

"No, really, Bro, I insist," said Dude. "After you."

"JUMP!" shouted Squirt at the top of his voice. "NOW!"

That did the trick. Dude set off first, closely followed by Bro. Scampering along the branch as fast as they could, they launched themselves into the air.

"WHEEEEE!" yelled Dude and Bro together, before landing in the neighbouring tree next to Squirt.

"That wasn't so bad, was it, Dude?" said Bro.

"Easy-peasy, lemon-squeezy, Bro!" replied Dude.

"Nice of you to drop in," said Squirt.

"Heh-heh-heh," chuckled Dude and Bro.

"I know what you're both thinking," said Squirt.

"You do?" said Bro.

"Awesome, mini-dude," said Dude. "Even *I* don't know what I'm thinking."

"You're thinking, why have we just jumped from one tree to another?" said Squirt.

Dude and Bro looked at each other and then at Squirt.

"So, why have we?" said Bro.

"Look," said Squirt, pointing.

"Where?" said Dude.

Squirt sighed. "Where I'm pointing!"

Dude and Bro looked. Squirt was pointing

at a wall below the tree. Not just any old wall, but the wall that ran round the whole of The Acacia Koala Sanctuary. The wall that kept unwelcome visitors from getting *in*. But perhaps, more importantly, the wall that stopped the sanctuary's residents from getting *out*.

"Follow me," said Squirt, starting to scramble down the trunk.

"Aw, come on, Squirt!" said Bro. "Can't we just stop and get our breath back for a bit?"

"I think you probably know the answer to that!" yelled Squirt.

"Yeah," muttered Bro. "I think I probably do."

"Heh-heh-heh," chuckled Dude, slipping and sliding down the trunk after Squirt. "Come on, Bro."

"Coming," said Bro.

Squirt was already sitting on top of the wall and peering over the edge by the time Dude and Bro caught up with him.

"Whoa," said Squirt.

"What is it?" asked Bro.

"I'm not sure I can climb down," said Squirt, nervously.

Dude and Bro peered over the edge too. It was a very high wall – but nowhere near as high as the tree they'd just climbed up and down. The problem was, unlike a tree, the wall was perfectly smooth with no branches or knobbly bits to cling to and use as paw-holds. One slip and it was a long way down!

"I see what ya mean," said Bro.

"Totally, mini-dude," said Dude.

The three koalas sat on the wall for a while, contemplating their next move. Well, Squirt was anyway. Exhausted from all the recent climbing and jumping, Dude and Bro had closed their eyes and were grabbing a quick forty winks.

Suddenly, Squirt spotted something. "Hey, look, guys!"

"Uh? What?" mumbled Bro sleepily.

"Look!" said Squirt, getting very excited. "Down there!"

Dude and Bro looked. A pick-up truck had stopped at some traffic lights below the wall where they were sitting. Loud rock music was blaring out of an open window. But that wasn't what Squirt was getting excited about. What Squirt was getting excited about was the pumped-up lilo in the back of the truck, next to a couple of surfboards.

"What about it?" said Dude.

"A bouncy thing!" squeaked Squirt, pointing to the lilo.

"Bouncy thing?" said Bro.

"Bouncy thing!" said Squirt. "Let's jump!"

"Awesome!" said Dude, fully awake. Or as awake as Dude ever got, that is.

"Ya reckon, Dude?" said Bro.

"Totally, Bro!" said Dude.

"Quick!" squeaked Squirt.

Before Dude and Bro could say another word, Squirt had launched himself into the air.

"Wheeeeeeeeeeeeeeeee!" yelled Squirt, before landing on the lilo, bouncing up and down a few times and eventually stopping.

"Wheeeeeeeeeeeeeeeee!" shouted Dude, doing exactly the same thing, causing Squirt to bounce up and down again.

Bro hesitated for just a second before eventually launching himself into the air too.

"Aaaaaaaaaaaaaaaaaaagh!" screamed Bro, before landing on the lilo – not only bouncing up and down himself, but causing Dude and Squirt to bounce up and down again as well.

"Er, Bro?" said Dude, once they'd all stopped bouncing about. "Did you say, 'Aaaaaaaaaaaaaaaaaaagh'?"

"Oops. Sorry, Dude," said Bro. "Obviously, I meant to say, 'Wheeeeeeeeeeeeeee'!"

"Heh-heh-heh," chuckled Dude.

"Right, guys, let's go!" urged Squirt, trying to scramble out the back of the truck.

"What?" said Bro.

"Well we can't stay in this thing," said Squirt.

"We can't?" said Dude.

"Do you know where it's heading?" said Squirt.

"No," said Dude.

"Exactly!" said Squirt. "Let's go!"

But before they had a chance to make a break for it, the lights turned green and the truck sped off.

Chapter Five

"Now what?" said Squirt as the pick-up truck containing not only surfboards and a lilo, but three stowaway koalas, zoomed down the road.

Bro shrugged. "Don't ask me."

"Well, I *am* asking you, actually," said

Squirt. "This is all *your* fault!"

"What are you talking about?" said Bro. "It's not my fault!"

Squirt glared at Bro. "If you'd been a bit quicker back there we could have hopped it before the lights changed!"

"Yeah, well..." began Bro.

"The little feller's right, Bro," said Dude.

"Who asked you?" snapped Bro.

Dude thought for a moment. "No one."

"In that case, keep yer big, fat nose out of this, Dude!" said Bro.

The truck really was going quite fast by now. Much too fast for the koalas to jump out. But where was it heading? That was the question.

"Sorry, Bro," said Dude.

"No worries, Dude," said Bro.

"Never mind that," said Squirt impatiently. "We've got to think!"

"Aw, mate," said Bro. "Do we really *have* to?"

"Heh-heh-heh," chuckled Dude.

Squirt sighed. "Come on! Concentrate here!"

"On what?" said Bro.

"Have a wild guess!" said Squirt.

Bro thought for a moment.

"Reckon he means yer baby sis, Bro," said Dude.

"Aw, yeah," said Bro.

But Squirt wasn't even listening any more.

He was too busy watching trees and buildings flash past. He was too busy watching traffic zoom by in the opposite direction. He was too busy watching people on the pavement, happily minding their own business and strolling around without a care in the world. And all the while Squirt was wondering, *Where is Squeak? What is she doing? Are we getting closer or further away from her?*

"D'ya reckon we're going the right way, mini-dude?" said Dude.

"That's the thing," said Squirt.

"What's the thing, Squirt?" asked Bro.

"I don't know," admitted Squirt.

"Uh?" said Dude. "You don't know what the thing is?"

"No!" said Squirt. "I don't know whether we're going the right way or not!"

"Heh-heh-heh," chuckled Bro.

"Well, I'm glad you think it's funny!" said Squirt.

"Sorry, Squirt," said Bro sheepishly. "I just don't know what to do."

"Well, that makes two of us," said Squirt.

"Three of us," added Dude.

The koalas rode on in silence for a while as the pick-up truck zoomed further and further away from The Acacia Koala Sanctuary. By now the sun was high in the sky. It was a long time till nightfall. Ma and Pa wouldn't be back from visiting Aunt Jemima for ages yet. If they found Squeak soon and hurried back, Mr and Mrs M need never even know she'd even been gone in the first place. But at the moment, that was looking like a mighty big *if*.

All of a sudden the truck began to slow down.

"Get ready!" squeaked Squirt.

"For what?" said Bro.

"To jump out!" yelled Squirt. "When we stop!"

"Whoa," said Dude. "Not sure that's such a great idea, mini-dude."

"Well, do you have a *better* idea?" asked Squirt.

If Dude *did* have a better idea, he didn't say what it was, because at that very moment the pick-up truck ground to a halt. Squirt looked. They'd stopped at some lights. Stationary traffic was queuing on either side of them. If they were going to make a break for it, they'd have to do it right now, before the traffic started to move again.

"WOOF!" said something very loud and close.

"AAAAAAAAAAGH!" screamed Dude and Bro and Squirt, diving for cover.

"WOOF! WOOF! WOOF!" said the something, even more loudly.

The three koalas peered gingerly over the back of the pick-up truck to see an enormous dog sitting in the car alongside, staring ferociously at them.

"Whoa!" said Bro. "I wouldn't like to get on *his* bad side, Dude!"

"I reckon we already *are* on his bad side, Bro," said Dude.

"Heh-heh-heh," chuckled Bro. "Reckon yer probably right there, Dude."

"Well, well, well," said an unfamiliar voice. "Will ya look at that, bro?"

"Uh? Look at what?" said Bro.

"Shhhhhhhhh!" hissed Squirt.

"Aw, cool, dude!" said another unfamiliar voice.

"Uh? What is?" said Dude.

"Shhhhhhhhh!" hissed Squirt again.

Dude, Bro and Squirt looked round to see two young guys in the cab of the pick-up truck turning round and smiling at them.

"Koala bears!" said the first guy.

"We're *not* bears!" muttered Bro grumpily.

"Shhhhhhhhh!" hissed Squirt for a third time. "Keep your voice down!"

"Wonder how they got there, dude?" said the second guy.

"Search me, bro," said the first.

Dude and Bro looked at each other in amazement.

"They've got the same names as you and me, Dude," said Bro.

"Awesome," said Dude.

"Awesome," said the second guy. "Hey, look out, dude, the lights are about to change!"

"Cool, bro," said the first guy. "In that case, it looks like these guys are coming with us!"

"Heh-heh-heh," chuckled the second guy. "Hope they can surf, dude!"

"Heh-heh-heh," chuckled the first guy as the traffic light turned from red to green and the pick-up truck began to pull away again.

"Hope we can what?" said Bro.

"Surf," said Squirt.

"Surf?" repeated Bro. "What's that?"

"No idea," said Squirt. "Looks like we're about to find out, though."

"Sounds cool to me," said Dude.

"Dude," said Bro. "Everything sounds cool to you."

"Heh-heh-heh," chuckled Dude.

The koalas sat back to enjoy the ride. Well, Squirt sat back to enjoy the ride. Dude and Bro lay back on the lilo to enjoy the ride. There was really nothing much else they could do. Not until the truck stopped, anyway. And the truck didn't look like it was about to stop anytime soon.

On and on they zoomed, past buildings of all shapes and sizes soaring into the sky. Gradually, though, the buildings got fewer and fewer and the sky gradually got bigger and bigger. Then, all of a sudden, they were whizzing through open countryside and leaving the city far behind. And still Squirt didn't know where they were going, or whether they were getting closer and closer to Squeak by the second – or further and further away! One thing was for sure – he'd never been this far from

The Acacia Koala Sanctuary before.

Dude sniffed. "Can you smell that, Bro?"

"Can I smell what, Dude?" said Bro.

Dude sniffed again. "That."

Bro sniffed. "Aw, yeah."

"What do ya suppose it is, Bro?" said Dude.

Bro sniffed again. "No idea, Dude. Never smelled anything like it before."

Squirt sniffed. He'd never smelled anything like it before, either. But whatever it was, there was plenty of it.

"Look!" yelled Dude.

"Where?" said Bro.

"There!" said Dude excitedly.

Squirt and Bro looked. Ahead was a

ribbon of blue between the land and the
sky, stretching as far as the eye could see.
The bluest blue they'd ever seen.

The ocean! They were heading for
the ocean!

"Whoa!" said Bro.

"Awesome!" agreed Dude.

"It's enormous!" breathed Squirt.

"Enormously awesome!" said Dude.

"That's what it is!" said Squirt.

"What what is?" asked Bro.

"The smell!" said Squirt. "It's the smell of the ocean!"

"Right," said Bro.

"Totally," said Dude.

Squirt was ecstatic. Not because they could see the ocean, but because he knew that wherever the ocean was, there was bound to be a beach nearby. And where there was a beach… well, Squirt was trying hard not to get *too* carried away, but it was beginning to look very much like they were at least getting *closer* to Squeak and not further away. It was a start. It was a big start!

How Squeak had managed to travel this far on her own was, of course, another matter altogether. But that wasn't important. Right now, all that mattered was finding Squeak and getting her back to The Acacia Koala Sanctuary as quickly as possible.

Chapter Six

The ribbon of blue gradually got bigger and bigger. The smell of the ocean gradually got stronger and stronger. In next to no time the pick-up truck was turning into a sandy car park full of other trucks, cars and camper vans – most of which were also carrying surfboards and blasting out loud music of one kind or another.

"The beach!" shouted Squirt.

"Cool!" said Bro.

"Awesome!" agreed Dude.

"Come on," said Squirt, hopping down on to the ground as soon as the truck had slowed to a halt.

"Where to?" said Bro, doing likewise.

"To find Squeak, of course!" said Squirt. "Look!"

"Where?" said Bro.

"Over there!" said Squirt, pointing towards a forest in the distance. "Kylie said she'd told Squeak about a big tree by the beach, didn't she!"

"Aw, yeah," said Bro.

"And look," said Squirt. "One of them does seem to be a lot bigger than the others."

Bro looked. "Aw, yeah, you're right, Squirt. D'ya reckon that could be the one?"

"Maybe," said Squirt, setting off. "Only one way to find out."

"Wait for me," said Bro, scurrying after him.

"Bye, little bear-dudes!" called one of the guys getting out of the pick-up. "Catch you later!"

"When will they learn?" grumbled Bro. "We're *not* bears!"

"Never mind that now!" said Squirt.

"We've got to find Squeak!"

Squirt and Bro started to run across the beach towards the forest. But it turned out to be much further away than it looked. Very soon the two koalas were puffed out and had to stop for a breather.

"I'm whacked," panted Bro.

"Me too," gasped Squirt.

"How about you, Dude?" said Bro.

There was no reply.

"Dude?" said Bro, turning round. But Dude wasn't there.

"Dude?" said Bro again. "Where are ya, mate?"

Squirt and Bro looked at each other anxiously. Where on earth had Dude got to? One minute he'd been there and the next he was gone. It was as if he'd vanished into thin air.

"This is getting ridiculous!" said Squirt. "First we lose Squeak and now Dude!"

"Dude!" called Bro. "Where are ya, mate?"

"He'd better not be hiding!" said Squirt crossly.

"If he is, then he's doing a pretty good job," said Bro.

"What do you mean?" asked Squirt.

"Well, can you see him?" said Bro.

Squirt shook his head. "No."

"Exactly!" chuckled Bro.

"It's *not* funny!" said Squirt.

"Sorry, Squirt," said Bro.

"I don't see how today could actually get any worse!" moaned Squirt.

"Dude!" called Bro. "Are you all right?"

But Dude was nowhere to be seen. Squirt and Bro looked at each other. What now? Should they look for him? Or should they carry on looking for Squeak and worry about Dude later?

There was a sudden squawk overhead. "Can I help?" cried a voice.

Squirt and Bro looked up to see a brilliant white seagull circling above.

"You look like you've lost something!"

"Not some*thing*!" said Squirt. "Some*one*!"

"Who?" shrieked the seagull.

"Dude!" said Bro.

"Dude?" repeated the seagull.

"Dude," said Bro.

"What does this *Dude* look like?" called the seagull.

Bro thought for a moment. "Erm… pretty much like me, I guess."

"And me," said Squirt.

Bro looked at Squirt. "But bigger."

"So a little bear, then," said the seagull.

"WE'RE NOT BEARS, WE'RE KOALAS!" yelled Bro.

"All right! All right!" squawked the seagull. "Do you want me to help you or not?"

"Sorry, mate," said Bro sheepishly.

"*Can* you help?" said Squirt.

"If I can't find her, no one can," said the seagull.

"Really?" said Squirt.

"Mate, I can spot half a cheese sarnie a mile off!"

"Seriously?" said Squirt.

"No worries," said the seagull. "With or without pickle."

"Heh-heh-heh," chuckled Bro.

"I can spot a burger bap in the next state!" said the seagull. "I can see a…"

"WHEEEEEEEEEEEEEEEEEEEE!!!" sang a familiar-sounding voice.

Squirt and Bro spun round to see Dude. To their astonishment he was in the ocean. To their even *greater* astonishment he was

zooming along on a wave, standing behind

one of the pick-up truck guys on a surfboard!

"Whoa!" exclaimed Bro. "Will ya look

at that?"

"A surfing koala?" said the seagull. "Now *there's* something I've never seen before!"

"So *that's* what surfing is!" said Squirt.

"Coooool!" said Bro.

Squirt and Bro watched as the wave got bigger and bigger and Dude and the guy began to zoom along faster and faster.

"AWESOOOOOOOOOOOME!!!" cried Dude.

"Dude!" yelled Bro, desperately trying to get his friend's attention. "Over here, mate!"

But Dude couldn't hear. By now the wave was truly enormous. The roar of the water filled the air.

"DUDE!" screamed Bro at the top of his voice.

This time Dude heard Bro all right. He turned round to see where he was. That was his first big mistake. His second big mistake was to wave to Bro. Waving on a wave turned out to be a bad idea. A *really* bad idea. Dude wobbled. And when he tried to correct the wobble, he wobbled even more.

Soon Dude was wobbling about like a particularly wobbly jelly on a plate. Squirt and Bro watched in horror from the beach as the wave finally broke and Dude was sent somersaulting high into the air, before landing in the water with a splash and disappearing.

"Oh my goodness!" cried Squirt. "Where's he gone?"

"Whoa," said Bro.

They waited and waited for Dude to reappear, getting more and more worried with each passing second.

"There he is!" squawked the seagull, spotting Dude as he finally

bobbed back up to the surface.

"Phew!" breathed Squirt.

"Thought he was a goner for a minute there, Squirt!" said Bro.

"He still might be!" screamed the seagull. "Look!"

Squirt and Bro looked. Zigzagging towards Dude through the water was something triangular.

"What's that, mate?" said Bro.

"You seriously don't know what that is?" said the seagull.

"I seriously don't, mate," said Bro. "And at this rate I'm not going to find out, either, am I? So if you wouldn't mind just spitting it out, it'll save an awful lotta time."

"It's a..." began the seagull as the triangle got closer and closer to Dude. "It's a..."

"What?" said Squirt, finally losing patience.

"SHARK!!!!" screeched the seagull.

Squirt and Bro looked at each other and shrugged. They had no idea what a shark was. But they were just about to find out.

"DUUUUUUUUDE!!!!" screamed Squirt as an enormous pointy snout full of enormous pointy teeth suddenly emerged from the water.

"SWIM FOR YER LIFE, MATE!" screamed Bro.

"Surfing's totally awesome, Bro!" yelled Dude, completely oblivious to the fact that a huge shark was bearing down on him and that it only seemed to have one thing on its mind. "You should totally try it sometime!"

"NEVER MIND SURFING, DUDE!" screamed Bro. "SWIM FOR IT! NOOOOOOW!!!"

"What?" said Dude, turning round and coming face to face with more teeth than he'd ever seen in one mouth before. And that included the crocodile back in The Acacia Koala Sanctuary.

"G'day, mate," said Dude cheerfully.

The shark stopped dead in its tracks. "G'day? What do you mean, *g'day?*"

"I mean, g'day, mate," said Dude. "How are ya?"

The shark was puzzled. "Aren't you scared of me?"

Dude thought for a moment. "No. Why? Am I s'posed to be?"

"Yes, you're supposed to be!" replied the shark indignantly. "You're supposed to be *terrified*!"

"Oh, right, I see," said Dude.

"I could gobble you up in one mouthful!" said the shark. "I could swallow you whole and you wouldn't even touch the sides!"

"Why would you want to do a thing like that?" asked Dude.

"Because I'm hungry?" said the shark.

"Oh, right," said Dude. "Fair enough. In that case I should probably get going."

The shark grinned, baring even *more* pointy teeth. "Yes, I think you probably should."

"Be seeing ya," said Dude, starting to paddle for the shore.

"You bet you will," grinned the shark, starting to swim after him.

"HURRY UP, DUUUUUUDE!!!" screamed Bro from the beach.

"I totally *am* hurrying, Bro!" yelled Dude.

"WELL, HURRY FASTER!!!" screamed Bro.

Squirt and Bro watched as Dude swam faster and faster. But the faster Dude swam,

the faster the shark followed.

"He's not going to make it!" squeaked Squirt.

"He's gonna make it, Squirt! He's gonna make it!" said Bro.

"DUDE! WATCH OUT!" screamed Squirt as the shark opened its jaws wide, ready to chomp down on the retreating koala.

But the shark had finally run out of ocean. Dude suddenly felt sand beneath his feet and scuttled up the beach just as fast as his little legs could carry him, before collapsing in a bedraggled, panting heap.

"You all right, Dude?" said Bro anxiously.

But Dude said nothing.

"Dude?" said Bro. "Speak to me, mate!"

Dude looked up at Bro. "Heh-heh-heh," he just about managed to pant.

"Heh-heh-heh," chuckled Bro, feeling mightily relieved.

"Grrrrrrr," grumbled the shark, eyeing the koalas hungrily.

Bro stuck his tongue out. "Better luck next time, goofy!"

"Heh-heh-heh," chuckled Dude, feeling better by the second.

Chapter Seven

"That was a pretty close call back there," said Squirt, scurrying along the beach towards the forest at the far end.

"Totally, mini-dude," said Dude, scurrying after him. "Totally."

"Heh-heh-heh," chuckled Bro, bringing up the rear.

Squirt turned round and shot Bro a disapproving look. "I really don't see what's so amusing! Dude very nearly got eaten by a shark just now!"

"He *nearly* got eaten by a shark," said Bro. "He didn't *actually* get eaten by a shark."

"That's hardly the point," said Squirt.

"Isn't it?" said Bro.

Squirt sighed. But it was useless arguing. Anyway, they still needed to find Squeak. And fast!

"You gotta admit, Dude," said Bro. "It *was* kinda funny."

"What was, Bro?" said Dude.

"When you came outta the water lookin' like a… like a…"

"Like a what, Bro?" asked Dude.

Bro thought for a moment. "Like a soggy wallaby."

"Heh-heh-heh," chuckled Dude, despite the fact that he'd never actually *seen* a soggy wallaby before. Then again, neither had Bro.

"What were you thinking, Dude?" said Squirt.

Dude was puzzled. "When I came out the water lookin' like a soggy wallaby, ya mean?"

"No!" said Squirt, getting frustrated. "When you went surfing!"

"Oh, right," said Dude. "Dunno. It just looked kinda fun I guess. And kinda cool too."

"Well, you shouldn't have gone off like that," scolded Squirt, striding ahead. "We're meant to be looking for Squeak! We're not meant to be having fun!"

"Sorry, mini-dude," said Dude. "Couldn't resist it."

"Don't blame ya, Dude," whispered Bro. "It did look kinda fun."

"I tell ya, mate, it was the best fun *ever*!" whispered Dude. "You should totally try it sometime!"

"I totally intend to, Dude," said Bro.

They walked on for a few more seconds.

"Can ya tell me something, Dude," said Bro.

"Go for it, mate," replied Dude.

"Were you *really* not scared of the shark?"

Dude turned to Bro. "Honestly, mate?"

"Honestly, mate," said Bro.

"I was absolutely petrified," said Dude.

"You were?" said Bro.

"Never been so scared in my life, Bro!" said Dude. "My heart was going like the clappers."

"Whoa!" said Bro.

"Why d'ya think I was swimming so fast?" said Dude.

"Heh-heh-heh," chuckled Bro. "You're a legend, Dude! A total legend!"

"Shhhhhhhh!" interrupted Squirt suddenly.

"What is it, Squirt?" said Bro.

"Listen!" said Squirt, stopping in his tracks.

Dude and Bro stopped and listened. They were too far away from the car park to hear the music blasting out of the camper vans and pick-up trucks any more. The only thing they could hear was the roar of the ocean.

"Can you hear it?" said Squirt.

"The ocean?" said Bro.

"Grrrrrrrrrrrrrrrrrr," growled something menacingly from the direction of the forest.

"No," said Squirt. "That growling noise."

Dude and Bro turned to each other. They could hear it all right. And whatever it was, it didn't sound particularly pleased to see them.

"Let's get outta here, Dude," said Bro.

"That sounds like an excellent idea, Bro," agreed Dude.

"Where do you think you're going?" demanded Squirt, as the other two turned round and began heading back in the direction they'd only just come from. "You can't turn back now!"

"I think you'll find we just did, Squirt," said Bro.

"What about Squeak?" said Squirt. "We can't just leave her here!"

Dude stopped. "Squirt's right, Bro."

Bro sighed and stopped too. "I know he's right."

"Grrrrrrrrrrrrrrrrrrrrrrrrrrrr!" growled the something again. "What do you want?"

The three koalas stared as a dingo stepped out of the shadows. Not only did it not *sound* particularly pleased to see Dude, Bro and Squirt, it didn't *look* particularly pleased, either.

"What are you doing on our beach?"

"*Our* beach?" said Bro. "But there's only one of you."

"Look again, Bro," whispered Dude, as a whole pack of dingoes slowly began to emerge from the trees and stand behind their leader.

"Er, hi!" said Squirt bravely, even though he was feeling anything but brave. "Sorry. Didn't realise it was your beach. We won't be long!"

"You're right," snarled the dingo. "You won't be."

The other dingoes cackled.

"Still wanna hang about, Squirt?" said Bro.

But Squirt just ignored Bro. "We're looking for someone, actually. I don't suppose you've seen her, have you?"

"Who?" said the dingo.

"Squeak," said Squirt.

"Squeak?" said the dingo.

Squirt nodded. "My little sister."

"So a bear, then," said the dingo.

"We're *not* bears!" muttered Bro.

Everything suddenly went very quiet. Even the ocean seemed to stop roaring.

"What did you just say?" said the dingo.

"Er, nothing," mumbled Bro.

"No, I definitely heard you say something," said the dingo.

Bro gulped. "I just said…"

"What?" said the dingo.

"We're not bears," said Bro quietly.

The dingo glared at Bro for a moment before suddenly bursting out laughing. A split second later, the other dingoes all burst out laughing too.

"*We're not bears!*" scoffed the dingo. "That's funny!"

But Bro said nothing.

"I said *that's funny*," said the dingo, continuing to glare at him.

"Heh-heh-heh," chuckled Bro nervously.

"Heh-heh-heh," chuckled Dude.

"So have you seen her, then?" said Squirt, keen to change the subject.

"Who?" said the dingo.

"My *sister*," said Squirt. "We're supposed to be looking after her while Ma and Pa visit Aunt Jemima."

"Oh, you are, are you?" said the dingo.

"Yes," said Squirt. "Ma said it was time we showed some responsibility."

"Oh, she did, did she?" said the dingo.

"And now we've gone and lost her," said Squirt.

"Oh, you have, have you?" said the dingo.

"So have you?" said Squirt.

"Have I what?" said the dingo.

"Seen her!" said Squirt, beginning to get quite annoyed.

"No," said the dingo. "But I know someone who *might* have seen her."

"Really?" said Squirt hopefully.

"No, not really," snarled the dingo before bursting out laughing, along with the rest of the pack.

Dude wasn't happy. Enough was enough. "There's no need for that, mate," he said.

"I beg your pardon?" said the dingo, clearly unused to anyone standing up to him.

"I said there's no need for that, mate," repeated Dude patiently. "That was just mean."

Everything suddenly went very quiet

again. What was the dingo going to do? The rest of the dingoes looked at their leader expectantly.

"You're absolutely right," said the dingo. "That was bang out of order of me. I'm very sorry."

"Really?" said Dude, surprised.

"No, not really," said the dingo, before bursting out laughing again, along with the others. "Now are you going to get off our beach, or are we going to make you?"

Dude and Bro looked at each other.

"What d'ya reckon, Dude?" said Bro. "Should we stay or should we go now?"

"What kind of a dumb question is that?" squeaked Squirt. "We've got to find Squeak!"

"He's right, ya know, Bro," said Dude.

"I *know* he's right!" snapped Bro. "Will ya stop saying that?"

"Well?" said the dingo. "We're waiting."

"So are we," said Squirt bravely.

"We've got all day," said the dingo.

"So have we," said Squirt, even though this wasn't strictly true. He and Dude and Bro needed to get back to The Acacia Koala Sanctuary, *with* Squeak, *before* Ma and Pa returned. It was a tall order. And with the sun already beginning to sink slowly towards the western horizon, it was getting taller by the second!

"Well, well," said the dingo.

"Well, well, well!" said Squirt.

"Heh-heh-heh," chuckled Bro.

But Dude said nothing. He'd had a sudden thought. And that didn't happen very often.

"Look!" he said.

"Where?" said the dingo.

"Up there!" said Dude, pointing to the sky.

The dingoes all looked up.

"What ya lookin' at, Dude?" said Bro, also looking up.

"Nothing!" whispered Dude.

Bro was puzzled. "Nothing? What d'ya mean, nothing?"

"Shhhhhhhh!" hissed Dude. "Run for it!"

"Huh?" said Bro, still puzzled.

"You heard him!" hissed Squirt. "Run for it!"

"Oh, right!" said Bro, finally twigging – and *finally* running for it.

Squirt and Dude had already managed to whiz past the dingoes without being noticed and had started to scramble up the nearest tree.

"HURRY UP, BRO!" yelled Dude.

That did it. The dingoes stopped looking up at the sky and immediately turned their attention towards Bro.

Bro looked at the dingoes. There was only thing for it.

"CHAAAAAAAAARGE!!!" yelled Bro as fiercely as he could, before putting a spurt on and whizzing even faster towards the tree.

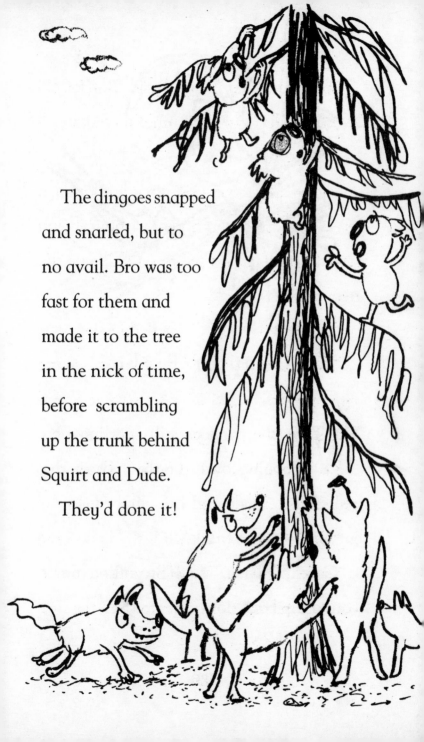

The dingoes snapped and snarled, but to no avail. Bro was too fast for them and made it to the tree in the nick of time, before scrambling up the trunk behind Squirt and Dude.

They'd done it!

Chapter Eight

With the dingoes still snarling and snapping away at the foot of the tree, Squirt, Dude and Bro climbed slowly but surely up the trunk.

"Careful, Dude," said Bro. "You don't wanna slip back down!"

"Too right I don't, Bro," said Dude, who'd only very recently had a close call with a none-too-friendly shark. He had no intention of having another one with a pack of angry-looking dingoes.

"Get back down here!" growled the leader.

"Yeah, right, mate!" said Bro. "In yer dreams!"

"Heh-heh-heh," chuckled Dude.

Even Squirt couldn't help smiling. It was such a relief to have got to the beach. And an even bigger relief to have avoided the snarling dingoes. Now all that remained was to find his little sister and take her home. If she was even here, of course.

They only had that crazy kookaburra's word that she was.

How long had it been since they'd last seen Squeak? wondered Squirt anxiously as he climbed higher and higher up the tree. Not since first thing that morning. And that was a long time ago now. *Was she OK? Had she eaten? What had she been up to all day?*

By now the dingoes were no more than dots on the ground. Snarling dots on the ground, but dots nevertheless. The koalas were safe – for the time being, anyway.

"Can I just say something?" said Dude.

"I dunno, Dude," said Bro. "Can you?"

"Heh-heh-heh," chuckled Dude. "Good one, Bro."

Squirt sighed. There was a time and a place for jokes and for larking around. This was neither the time, nor the place. "Go on, Dude. What were you going to say?"

"Aw, yeah," said Dude. "I was just going to say – aren't we supposed to be lookin' for the *tallest* tree?"

"Correct," answered Squirt.

"Right," said Dude. "Only this tree we're climbing up isn't actually the tallest."

"It isn't?" said Bro.

"No, mate," said Dude. "That's the tallest tree over there."

"Where, mate?" said Bro.

"There, mate," said Dude with a tilt of his head – afraid that if he was to let go of the trunk in order to point, he might slip all the way back down to the bottom again.

"Aw, yeah," said Bro. "I see what ya mean."

Squirt looked and immediately saw that Dude was right. They'd obviously been in such a mad rush to avoid the dingoes, they'd simply shot up the *nearest* tree. And the *nearest* tree wasn't the *tallest* tree. Squirt was surprised that *he* hadn't noticed this himself. But even more surprised that Dude *had*.

"Bummer," said Bro.

"Totally," said Dude.

"I'll tell ya something I *have* noticed though, Dude," said Bro.

"What's that, Bro?" asked Dude.

"Look what kind of tree this is!"

Dude glanced around. It suddenly dawned on him. They were in a eucalyptus tree!

"Aw, ya beauty!" said Dude. "What are we waiting for?"

Dude and Bro quickly scrambled the rest of the way up to the treetop. By the time Squirt joined them they were already tucking in.

"What do you think you're doing?" squeaked Squirt in disbelief.

"What does it *look* like?" said Bro between mouthfuls.

"It looks like you've forgotten what we're here for!" said Squirt. "*That's* what it looks like!"

"What?" said Bro. "No way, Squirt. Just a quick pit stop, that's all."

"Aw, yeah," said Dude. "Just takin' on

a bit of fuel, that's all, mate. Just recharging the old batteries."

"But we've got to find Squeak!" said Squirt.

"Totally, mate," agreed Dude. "And we will."

"Just as soon as we've chowed down a few more eucy leaves," said Bro.

"Unbelievable," groaned Squirt.

"You're not wrong," said Bro. "They *are* unbelievable."

"Totally delicious," said Dude.

"Try one," said Bro.

"Seriously?" said Squirt.

"Seriously, mini-dude," said Dude. "You totally won't regret it."

Squirt sighed. Perhaps Dude and Bro were right. Perhaps they *did* need to recharge their batteries a bit. It had been a long day and there was still plenty of it left. This might be the one and only opportunity they got to eat. It needn't take long. And he *was* hungry.

Squirt took a branch and started to chew on a leaf. "Whoa!"

"See," said Bro.

"Told you it was delicious, mini-dude," said Dude.

"Mmmmm," said Squirt. "I didn't know it would be quite *this* delicious!"

"Heh-heh-heh," chuckled Dude.

"Heh-heh-heh," chuckled Bro.

The three koalas lay back in the treetop, each chewing their eucalyptus branch, each beginning to feel more and more relaxed – and each starting to feel just… a little… bit… sleepy.

"STOP!" yelled Squirt, so suddenly and so loudly that Dude and Bro very nearly fell out of the tree.

"Whoa, chillax, mini-dude," said Dude.

"Chillax?" said Squirt. "That's precisely what we *can't* do! We've got to focus here!"

"What?" said Bro.

"Concentrate!" said Squirt. "Come up with a plan!"

"Plan?" said Bro.

"Look how far it is to the tallest tree!"

Dude and Bro looked.

"Well?" said Squirt. "Notice anything?"

"It's a long way," said Dude.

"Exactly!" said Squirt. "Much too far to jump this time!"

"Phew!" said Bro, recalling when they'd had to leap from one tree to another, back home in The Acacia Koala Sanctuary. "Thank goodness for that!"

"Heh-heh-heh," chuckled Dude.

"So, what now?" said Bro.

"Don't ask me, Bro," said Dude.

"I wasn't asking you, Dude," said Bro. "I was asking Squirt."

"Oh, right," said Dude.

"No offence, mate," said Bro.

"None taken, Bro," said Dude.

"We've got to go back down," said Squirt.

Dude and Bro looked at each other for a moment.

"Sorry, Squirt. You'll have to repeat that," said Bro. "For a minute there I thought you said we'd have to go back down."

"I did," said Squirt.

"No way!" protested Bro. "We can't do that!"

"What choice do we have?" said Squirt.

"He's—" began Dude.

"I KNOW HE'S RIGHT, DUDE!" yelled Bro, cutting Dude off.

"Well, then," said Dude, "what are we waiting for?"

"What are we waiting for?" said Bro. "I'll tell you what we're waiting for, Dude. We're waiting for those… those…"

"Dingoes to go?" said a voice from above.

"Yeah," said Bro. "Dingoes to go."

Squirt was puzzled. "Who said that?"

"Me," said the voice.

Squirt, Dude and Bro looked up to see a kookaburra sitting on a branch, looking back down at them.

"Mwah, ha ha ha ha!" screeched the bird. "That had you going, didn't it!"

"You must be Kyle," sighed Squirt.

"That's right, mate," said Kyle. "How d'ya know that?"

"We know your cousin Kylie," said Squirt. "We live in The Acacia Koala Sanctuary."

"G'day," said Kyle. "How's it going?"

"Not very well, actually," said Squirt.

"Oh?" said Kyle. "And why's that, then?"

"We need to get to that tree over there," said Squirt, with a nod of his head.

"The really tall one?" asked Kyle.

"Exactly," said Squirt.

"So what's the problem?" said Kyle.

"We can't fly, mate," said Bro. "That's the problem."

"Heh-heh-heh," chuckled Dude.

"Oh, right, I see," said Kyle. "So that's

why you're waiting for the dingoes to go!"

"Exactly," said Squirt again.

Kyle thought for a moment. "Hmmm. I think I might just be able to help."

"Really?" said Squirt.

"Sure. Why not," said Kyle. "You seem like nice enough bears to me."

Squirt glared at Bro.

"Thank you," said Bro through gritted teeth. "That would be amazing."

"No worries," said Kyle. "Now I just need a stick."

"A stick?" said Squirt.

"Dogs can't resist sticks," said Kyle.

"Dogs?" said Squirt. "But I thought you said they were dingoes!"

"Mwah, ha ha ha ha!" laughed Kyle. "Dingoes. Dogs. Same thing!"

"Here ya go, mate," said Dude, holding up a branch that, until recently, had been covered in juicy eucalyptus leaves.

"Perfect!" said Kyle, hopping down from his perch and grabbing the stick with both feet. "Now when I say '*Fetch!*' – you *go!* Got me?"

"Got you," said Squirt.

"Fetch?" said Bro. "What's he talkin' about, Dude?"

"No idea, Bro," said Dude.

"Just do what he says!" urged Squirt.

And with that, Kyle suddenly swooped out of sight.

Squirt, Dude and Bro peered down below to see what was going on. To their astonishment, the dingoes appeared to be sitting obediently and hanging on Kyle's every word.

"Stay!" screeched Kyle, flying round and round, still holding the stick in his feet. "Good doggies!"

"Wait for it," said Squirt.

"Wait for what?" said Bro, by now thoroughly confused.

"FETCH!" screeched Kyle, zooming off with the stick and immediately being pursued by the entire pack of dingoes, all yapping and barking excitedly.

"GO, GO, GO!" squeaked Squirt, half climbing, half sliding down the tree trunk just as fast as he could manage without falling.

"But…" said Bro.

"Just do it, Bro! Just do it!" yelled Dude, following Squirt.

"Coming, Dude!" yelled Bro, leaping into action.

By the time the three koalas reached the foot of the tree, the dingoes had disappeared completely.

"Quick! Before they come back!" cried Squirt, dashing across the ground towards the tallest tree.

"Right behind ya, Squirt!" said Bro, dashing after his little brother.

"Totally, mini-dude!" said Dude, dashing after Bro.

They were up the tree like a shot. And

this time it really *was* the tallest tree! Higher and higher they climbed. And the higher they climbed, the more they had to stop and rest. Each time they stopped, they called out.

"Squeak? Squeak? You up there?"

But each time there was no reply. And each time there was no reply, Squirt, Dude and Bro got a little bit more worried. Was Squeak up there? If so, why was she not answering? Was she hurt? What had happened?

And then at long, long last – just when they were about to give up hope altogether, they spotted something. A tiny shape, wedged between the skinniest of branches, at the very top of the tree.

"There she is!" yelled Squirt.

"Aw, yeah!" panted Bro breathlessly. "Squeak? You all right, mate?"

"Speak to us, mini-mini-dude!" panted Dude.

But still there was no reply. The three koalas looked at each other anxiously.

"Wait here," said Squirt, starting to climb again. "I'm only small. I can make it to the top, I know I can!"

"Good on ya, Squirt!" panted Bro.

"Totally," panted Dude.

Dude and Bro watched as Squirt climbed to the very top of the very tallest tree, more and more afraid of what he might find when he got there. They waited… and waited… and waited… until eventually Squirt shouted something. But he was so high up his voice was carried away in the wind.

"What was that, Squirt?" yelled Bro.

Squirt shouted again.

"Sorry, mate, you'll have to shout louder than that!" bellowed Bro.

"SHE'S OK!" shouted Squirt at the very top of his voice, from the very top of the tree. "SHE'S JUST ASLEEP!"

Dude and Bro turned to each other.

"Asleep?" said Dude.

"I bet she's not any more, Dude," said Bro.

"Heh-heh-heh," chuckled Dude. "I bet she's not, either, Bro."

Chapter Nine

Bro was absolutely right. Squeak woke up the second that Squirt began to shout.

"Hey, sis," smiled Squirt as soon as she opened her eyes.

Squeak blinked a couple of times, almost

as if she didn't quite know where she was. Which was probably just as well because where Squeak was, any sudden movement could have meant curtains – not only for her, but for Squirt as well.

"It's me," said Squirt gently. "Squirt."

Squeak blinked a couple more times before the penny finally dropped.

"Yeah! Squirty-wirty! Squirty-wirty!" she squeaked excitedly, leaping to her feet and throwing herself at her brother.

"Whoa! Careful now, Squeak!" warned Squirt. "It's a long way down!"

"Big tree! Big tree!" sang Squeak, bouncing up and down and making the branch bounce up and down too.

"Yes," said Squeak. "Big tree. But it's time to climb down now."

"Poo, poo!" said Squeak, still bouncing up and down. "Poo, poo! Poo, poo!"

Squirt couldn't help laughing, despite the fact that by now the branch was wobbling about quite alarmingly. He was just glad to have found his little sister at last.

"Come on. Let's go."

"Leaf!" said Squeak.

"Yes, that's right. We've got to leave," said Squirt.

"No! Leaf, leaf!" squeaked Squeak. "Leaf, leaf!"

"What?" said Squirt.

"Leaf for Bro-bro!" squeaked Squeak. "Leaf for Bro-bro!"

"Oh, right!" said Squirt. "*Leaf!*"

What with everything else that had been going on, Squirt had quite forgotten that that was why Squeak had gone missing in the first place. She'd been sent on a mission by Bro. And she still seemed very determined to complete it.

"Wait a minute," said Squirt, reaching as high as he could to pick a leaf.

"Me do it! Me do it!" said Squeak.

Before Squirt could stop her, Squeak had scrambled up on to his shoulders and had plucked a leaf herself.

"Yeah! Leaf for Bro-bro!" squeaked Squeak. "Leaf for Bro-bro!"

Squirt could scarcely believe what was happening. Here he was, higher than he'd ever been before in his life – and his little sister was even higher! Ma and Pa would go bonkers if they ever found out. Which reminded Squirt that they really ought to get going. He had no idea how they were going to get back to the sanctuary – or how long it would take to get there.

"Time to go, Squeak," urged Squirt gently.

"Poo, poo!" said Squeak.

"Sorry, sis. Down you get," said Squirt.

Squeak reluctantly did as she was told and hopped off Squirt's shoulders.

"Follow me," said Squirt, starting to climb slowly back down the tree. "And for goodness' sake be careful!"

"Poo, poo," said Squeak, but following anyway.

***

"Thought you two had got lost up there," said Bro when Squirt and Squeak eventually joined him and Dude on the branch where they'd been resting.

"Yeah! Leaf for Bro-bro! Leaf for Bro-bro!" squeaked Squeak, handing Bro the leaf.

"Aw, thanks, Squeak," said Bro. "You really shouldn't have."

"Heh-heh-heh," chuckled Dude.

"Yeah! Dudey-wudey! Dudey-wudey!" squeaked Squeak.

"Come on, guys!" said Squirt, carrying on down the tree.

"Coming," said Bro.

"Totally," agreed Dude.

"Poo, poo!" said Squeak.

"Heh-heh-heh," chuckled Dude and Bro together.

But Squirt wasn't paying any attention. All he was concerned about was getting home before Ma and Pa did.

"Hurry up, you three!" he yelled as he

reached the ground and scurried off back towards the beach.

"No worries, Squirt!" shouted Bro, sliding down the last bit of the trunk.

"Wheeeee!" cried Dude, doing the same and landing on top of Bro.

"Wee-wee! Wee-wee!" squeaked Squeak, landing in a heap on top of Dude *and* Bro.

"Heh-heh-heh," chuckled Dude and Bro, getting up and dusting themselves down.

But by now the sun was sinking fast. The shadows of the trees were stretching longer and longer. The forest was getting gloomier by the minute.

"Where did he go?" said Bro.

"Who?" said Dude.

"Who d'ya think, ya wallaby?" said Bro. "Squirt!"

"Oh, right," said Dude, looking around. "Erm…"

"Squirt?" shouted Bro. "Where are ya, mate?"

"Yeah! Squirty-wirty! Squirty-wirty!" squeaked Squeak.

"Grrrrrrrrrrrrrrrrrrrrrrrrrr!" growled something in the dark.

Dude and Bro looked at each other anxiously. The dingoes!

"Let's get outta here, Dude," said Bro.

"Totally, Bro," agreed Dude.

"Which way?" said Bro.

"This way!" squawked Kyle, suddenly

appearing and then disappearing almost as quickly. "Follow me! Quick!"

"Hop on!" said Dude urgently.

"Are ya sure, Dude?" said Bro. "I'm heavier than ya think."

"Not you, Bro!" said Dude. "I was talkin' to Squeak!"

"Yeah! Dudey-wudey! Dudey-wudey!" squeaked Squeak, scrambling up on to Dude's back.

"GRRRRRRRRRRRRRR!" growled the dingoes again, much louder – and this time clearly *much* nearer!

That did it. Dude and Bro shot off as fast as they could, doing their best not to lose sight of Kyle as he whizzed and fluttered in between the trees. Ahead, they could just make out another shape, scurrying along in the gloom.

"SQUIRT!" yelled Bro. "WAIT FOR US!"

"YEAH! SQUIRTY-WIRTY! SQUIRTY-WIRTY!" squeaked Squeak at the top of her voice.

As Dude and Bro raced through the forest, it gradually got lighter and lighter until eventually they burst out on to the beach.

"What kept you?" asked Squirt.

"Mwah, ha ha ha ha!" screeched Kyle. "*What kept you?* That's funny!"

"Glad you think so," muttered Bro.

"You should be grateful," said Squirt. "If it wasn't for Kyle here, you might still be in the forest!"

"He's right, you know, Bro," said Dude.

Bro turned to Dude, but before he could say anything there was an almighty snarling sound behind them. They looked round to see the dingoes standing at the edge of the forest.

"RUN!" screeched Kyle.

The koalas didn't need telling twice. They ran and they kept on running until they couldn't run any further, before collapsing in a heap on the sand.

"Phew!" panted Squirt. "That was *another* close call!"

"Yeah, thanks, mate," panted Dude to Kyle, who was still fluttering around above them. "Dunno what we'd have done without ya."

"No worries," said Kyle. "Glad to be of service!"

"Seriously, Kyle, mate, we owe ya one," puffed Bro.

"Well, you never know, I might just drop by next time I pay my cousin Kylie a visit," said Kyle.

"Yeah! Kyley-wiley! Kyley-wiley!" squeaked Squeak.

"Heh-heh-heh," chuckled Dude and Bro, together.

"Hey! Look, Bro!" said a familiar voice a few moments later. "It's the little bear-dudes! And check it out – here's a baby bear-dude too!"

Squirt, Dude, Bro *and* Squeak looked up to see the guys from the pick-up truck wandering past, carrying their surfboards underneath their arms. The koalas were still too exhausted to move – and in the case of Bro, still too exhausted to be cross about being called a bear.

"Hey! How's it going, bear-dudes?" said one of them. "You guys need a lift?"

The koalas looked at each other. A *lift*? You bet they needed a lift!

"Follow us, bear-dudes," said the other pick-up truck guy, heading back along the beach towards the car park.

"Go for it!" laughed Kyle.

Mustering up all the energy they had left, Squirt, Dude, Bro and Squeak got to their feet and scurried along behind the pick-up truck guys.

They were on their way home!

Chapter Ten

By the time the four koalas had reached the pick-up truck and hopped in the back, the sun was already beginning to dip behind a hill. By the time the pick-up truck had left the car park and started to zoom back towards the city, Squirt, Dude, Bro and

Squeak were already struggling to keep their eyes open. They soon stopped even trying. It had been a long, tiring day after all. And it wasn't over yet. They figured they might as well grab a quick snooze while they could. Well, Squirt figured he might as well grab a snooze while he could. The others just grabbed one anyway.

Before they knew it – or rather, before they *didn't* know it – they'd fallen fast asleep and the truck was rumbling through the suburbs. Buildings began to spring up on either side of the road and the traffic gradually got heavier and heavier.

BEEEEEEEEEP! went a car horn all of a sudden.

"What was that?" yawned Bro.

"What was what?" yawned Dude.

BEEEEEEEEP! went the car horn again.

"That," said Bro.

"A car," said Squirt, wide awake. "We must be getting close to the city."

"Yeah! Beepy-weepy! Beepy-weepy!" squeaked Squeak, also wide awake.

"Heh-heh-heh," chuckled Dude and Bro.

Squirt gazed ahead, trying to see if they were anywhere near The Acacia Koala Sanctuary. But it wasn't easy. By now it really was quite dark. If it wasn't for the lights of the pick-up truck itself, he would hardly have been able to see anything at all.

But that, figured Squirt, was the *least* of

their problems. If, and when, they eventually got back to the sanctuary – and Ma and Pa had already beaten them to it – they were going to be in *real* trouble! He and Dude and Bro had been left to look after Squeak, and they'd failed miserably. OK, so they'd found her in the end – and thank goodness she'd been safe and well – but they should never have lost her in the first place! What would Ma and Pa say? What would they do?

"Does anyone know where we are?" asked Squirt. "Because I don't!"

Bro suddenly burst out laughing.

"Oh, so you think that's funny, do you?" said Squirt.

"What?" said Bro. "No, no! I wasn't

laughing at that, Squirt. Stop it, Squeak!"

Squirt turned round to see Squeak tickling Bro's ears.

"Yeah! Tickle Bro-bro!" squeaked Squeak. "Tickle Bro-bro! Tickle Bro-bro!"

"Ha ha ha ha!" laughed Bro. "Seriously, Squeak! Stop doing that, will ya?"

"Squeak!" said Squirt sternly. "Stop it, now!"

Squeak stopped and looked at Squirt for a moment before starting to sob softly. Squirt was immediately horrified.

"I didn't mean to make you cry!"

Squeak sniffed a couple of times.

"Cuddles?" said Squirt, arms out wide.

"Yeah! Cuddly-wuddly! Cuddly-wuddly!"

squeaked Squeak, throwing herself at Squirt
and almost knocking him off his feet.

"I'm sorry, Squeak,"
said Squirt, hugging
his little sister
tightly. "Are we
friends now?"

"Yeah! Squirty-
wirty and Squeaky-
weaky!" said Squeak.

"Heh-heh-heh," chuckled Bro.

"Anyone know where we are yet?" said
Dude.

"What's that, mate?" said Bro.

"Well, we can't be nowhere," said Dude.
"We've gotta be somewhere."

"Very true, Dude," said Bro. "Very true."

Squirt continued to gaze ahead until, after a while, something loomed into view. Something *very* familiar looking.

"We're here!" yelled Squirt.

"We're always here, if you think about it, mini-dude," said Dude.

"No, I mean we're actually *here*!" yelled Squirt. "Look! The wall!"

Dude and Bro looked. The pick-up truck had stopped at some traffic lights – the traffic lights right outside The Acacia Koala Sanctuary!

"Aw, yeah," exclaimed Bro.

"Awesome," said Dude.

"Yeah!" squeaked Squeak.

"Quick! Let's go!" yelled Squirt hopping out the back of the truck.

The others didn't need telling twice and immediately hopped out of the truck as well. It was a good job they did too, as the next moment the lights turned green and the truck set off down the road again.

"Bye, surfer-dudes!" yelled Dude.

"Thanks for the lift!" shouted Bro.

"Yeah! Lifty-wifty! Lifty-wifty!" squeaked Squeak.

"Heh-heh-heh," chuckled Dude and Bro.

But Squirt was busy thinking. Now that they'd somehow managed to find their way back to The Acacia Koala Sanctuary, how were they actually going to get inside? They couldn't simply climb over the wall, for the same reason that they couldn't climb down it earlier. It was much too high and smooth, with nothing to cling on to. Koalas are great climbers, but not *that* great!

They couldn't try and sneak in the main entrance, either. The main entrance was closed and it was dark now. All the visitors had gone home!

Wait a minute, thought Squirt. *What about that gate at the side of the sanctuary?* The one they'd sneaked out of the time the rest of the koalas had transferred to the big zoo and he and Dude and Bro had got left behind?

"This way, guys!" said Squirt, scuttling along the bottom of the wall.

"Where are you going?" asked Bro.

"Follow me and find out!" said Squirt.

"Yeah! Squirty-wirty! Squirty-wirty!" squeaked Squeak, doing exactly what Squirt suggested.

Dude and Bro looked at each other and shrugged, before hurrying after Squirt and Squeak. By the time they caught up, the two youngsters had whizzed round a corner and were hiding in a bush.

"Shhhhhhh!" hissed Squirt, as Dude and Bro approached.

"What's going on, mini-dude?" whispered Dude, walking over to the bush.

"Look!" whispered Squirt.

Dude and Bro looked. In the gathering

gloom they could just about make out the shape of a keeper's buggy parked next to the wall while the keeper opened the gate.

"If we're very quick, we can do it!" whispered Squirt. "Come on!"

Without waiting for the others to answer, Squirt set off towards the gate. There wasn't a moment to lose. Not if they wanted to nip through before it closed again.

Dude, Bro and Squeak scurried after Squirt as fast as they could. As they did so, the keeper got into the buggy and drove into the sanctuary, before stopping again in order to close the gate behind him. The koalas hurried through and hid behind a rubbish bin. A split second later, the gate clanked shut. And because it was so dark, the keeper was none the wiser.

They'd done it! They were back in The Acacia Koala Sanctuary!

"Heh-heh-heh," chuckled Dude and Bro together.

"Shhhhhhhh!!!" hissed Squirt.

"Hello?" said the keeper. "Anyone there?"

"Poo, poo!" said Squeak.

"Who said that?" asked the keeper anxiously.

Squirt glared at Squeak, desperately hoping that she wouldn't say anything else. And for once she didn't. Somewhere in the trees above, an owl hooted.

"Strange," said the keeper to himself as

he climbed back into the buggy. "Must've imagined it."

The four koalas watched as the buggy drove away.

"Come on, guys!" said Squirt, zooming off again as soon as it had disappeared.

"I had a feeling he was going to say that, Dude," said Bro, following Squirt.

"Me too, Bro," said Dude, following Bro.

"Yeah Homey-womey!" squeaked Squeak, following all three of them.

***

In next to no time, Squirt, Dude, Bro and Squeak were scrambling up to their treetop. But what would they find when they reached it? Would Ma and Pa have got there first?

They didn't have to wait long to find out the answer. And the answer was…

No! The treetop was perfectly empty! Miraculously, they'd somehow made it back before Ma and Pa!

"YES!" shouted Squirt. "WE DID IT! WE DID IT! WE DID IT!"

"Did what?" said Ma, suddenly appearing.

"Erm, nothing, Ma," said Squirt as casually as possible. "Just showed some… some…"

Squirt stopped. What was that big long word Ma had used?

"Responsibility?" said Ma.

Squirt nodded. "Yes. Responsibility."

"Heh-heh-heh," chuckled Dude and Bro, already chowing down on a couple of eucalyptus branches.

"What's going on?" asked Ma suspiciously, just as Pa appeared in the treetop.

"Nothing, Ma," said Squirt. "Everything's fine."

"So a nice quiet day, then, boys?" said Pa with a wink.

Squirt nodded again. "Nice and quiet, Pa. Nice and quiet."

"How's your little sister been?" said Ma.

"As good as gold, Ma!" said Squirt. "Haven't you, Squeak?"

They turned towards the youngest koala. But Squeak was already curled up, fast asleep. Or at least it looked like she was, anyway.

"Beachy-weechy," murmured Squeak. "Beachy-weechy."

"Beachy-weechy?" said Ma.

"Oh, don't pay any attention, Ma," said Squirt. "She's obviously just dreaming."

"Heh-heh-heh," chuckled Dude and Bro.

"Hmm," said Ma. "Well, it's high time

you three were asleep too."

"Good idea, Ma," said Bro, stretching and yawning.

"Totally," said Dude, doing the same.

"Night, Ma. Night, Pa," said Squirt, snuggling down next to Squeak. The day, which hadn't started with a bang, was ending without a bang too. And that was just fine as far as Squirt was concerned.

"Night, boys," said Pa, giving Squirt, Dude and Bro another wink.

Awesome Animals

Awesome adventures with the wildest wildlife!

COMING IN 2013!
OTTER CHAOS – THE DAM BUSTERS
LLAMA DRAMA – IN IT TO WIN IT!
ENGUIN PANDEMONIUM – CHRISTMAS CRACKERS

Meet more
AWESOME ANIMALS!

For awesome videos and competitions go to:

www.awesomeanimalsbooks.com